FACTS AND FICTION ABOUT DRUGS™

I0808902

ALCOHOL

AVERY ELIZABETH HURT

rosen publishing's rosen central

New York

In loving memory of Margaret Helen Jones. She was stronger than alcohol. But then, she was stronger than most things.

Published in 2020 by The Rosen Publishing Group, Inc.
29 East 21st Street, New York, NY 10010

First Edition

Cataloging-in-Publication Data

Names: Hurt, Avery Elizabeth, author.
Title: Alcohol / Avery Elizabeth Hurt.
Description: First edition. | New York : Rosen Publishing, 2020. | Series: Facts and fiction about drugs | Audience: Grades 5–8. | Includes bibliographical references and index.
Identifiers: ISBN 9781725347564 (library bound) | ISBN 9781725347540 (pbk.)
Subjects: LCSH: Drinking of alcoholic beverages—Juvenile literature. | Teenagers—Alcohol use—Juvenile literature. | Alcoholism—Prevention—Juvenile literature.
Classification: LCC HV5066.H87 2020 | DDC 613.81—dc23

Manufactured in the United States of America

CONTENTS

INTRODUCTION

On its web page "The Science Inside Alcohol Project," the American Association for the Advancement of Science (AAAS) tells the story of kids whose lives have been affected by alcohol. Sandy is one of these children. Sandy had a loving family and plenty of friends. When he entered high school, he changed schools. He had trouble fitting in on the new, larger campus. He became shy and awkward. Then he discovered alcohol. When he drank, he felt more confident and outgoing. However, Sandy soon learned that alcohol wasn't solving his problems. Drinking was just creating more. Alcohol abuse can damage a person's health, relationships, and future. Fortunately for Sandy, his parents knew what to do. They enrolled him in a treatment program where he learned to deal with his problems without alcohol.

Alcoholism or alcohol use disorder (AUD) is a very common illness. The National Institute for Alcohol Abuse and Alcoholism (NIAAA) collects data about this disease. According to the NIAAA, fifteen million American adults have AUD. So do more than six hundred thousand people between the ages of twelve and seventeen.

In all fifty US states, drinking or purchasing alcohol is illegal for anyone under twenty-one years old. In Canada, the legal drinking age is nineteen in most of the country. (In the provinces of Alberta, Manitoba, and Québec, that age is eighteen.) There is a good reason for these limits. Alcohol is very dangerous for young people. Among other things, alcohol abuse can cause lasting brain damage.

Hundreds of thousands of young people have alcohol use disorder (AUD), which can have a negative effect on every part of their lives.

Alcohol isn't all bad, though. Yes, it is a drug, but it is also a drink that is enjoyed as a part of meals. Responsible adults can use alcohol safely. Wine, beer, and spirits play a role in society from religious ceremonies to fine dining. Used in moderation, alcohol may even have a few health benefits for adults. But for kids and teens, alcohol is never safe.

In order to make good decisions about whether or not to drink alcohol, people need to know what alcohol is, how it affects the body, and how it affects people's lives. And that is an interesting story that starts a very long time ago.

CHAPTER ONE

Alcohol in History

People have used alcohol for a long time and for many different reasons. Throughout history, alcohol has played a role in doctors' offices, houses of worship, and on family dinner tables. It has caused both joy and suffering. It has been both cherished and banned. Alcohol's double role as a part of meals and an often-dangerous drug has given it a complex role in history.

Remedies and Rituals

Alcohol is made from fruits, vegetables, or grains. Yeast or bacteria turn the sugars in these foods into alcohol. This chemical process is called fermentation. Fermentation often happens naturally to rotting fruits and grains. People also make alcohol by this same process. They brew beer and ale. They make wine. They distill liquors, such as whiskey, gin, and vodka.

This distillery in Kentucky makes bourbon from a mixture of corn and other grains. Other distilled liquors include whiskey, brandy, rum, and vodka.

No one knows when alcohol was first discovered. Some experts think it may have been discovered by accident. Perhaps someone tasted a piece of rotting fruit that had begun to ferment. They liked the taste. They liked the way it made them feel. And that was the beginning of a long and complicated relationship between humans and alcohol.

Historians may not know exactly how alcohol was discovered, but they do know that people have been using it for a very long time. According to a paper published in the *Proceedings of the National Academy of Scientists*, in 2004, scholars found evidence of alcohol use in the ruins of a Stone Age village. The village was nine thousand years old. In 2018, according to a report in the *Times of Israel*, archeologists found a thirteen-thousand-year-old brewery in a cave in Israel. Some experts think that humans have always eaten or drunk fermented foods and beverages.

Throughout history, people have used alcohol for many different purposes. For many years, alcohol was used as medicine. Doctors gave it to patients to relieve pain. It was used to treat snake bites and to clean wounds. Before antibiotics were developed, alcohol was one of the few ways to prevent infection.

Wine was commonly used by physicians for many years. Hippocrates was a physician in ancient Greece. He is often called the Father of Medicine. Hippocrates created a remedy for intestinal worms. It was a mixture of herbs and wine. Most physicians at that time relied heavily on wine for medicine. Doctors were still using alcohol of various kinds until the early twentieth century. However, by the 1900s, scientists had discovered better medicines. Doctors gradually stopped giving their patients alcohol.

The matzoh, nuts, and wine shown here are a traditional part of the Jewish celebration of Passover. Many faiths include alcohol in their religious rituals.

Alcohol has also been used for religious ceremonies. In ancient times, alcohol was often used by shamans or other religious leaders. Today views about alcohol vary among religions. Islam forbids alcohol. Buddhism discourages its use. Some religions permit alcohol and even make use of it in religious ceremonies. Wine plays a significant role in some Jewish and Christian rituals. For Jews, Sabbath and holiday meals usually begin with the kiddush. This is a formal blessing of wine. It is performed before the blessing of the bread. In Christian churches, worshippers often drink wine as a part of the communion ceremony.

Still, most religions either forbid or caution against the use of alcohol outside of religious settings. Partaking of small amounts of wine during religious services is allowed. Some religions allow adults to drink moderate amounts of alcohol socially. But in most religions, of course, drunkenness is frowned upon and is often considered sinful.

Today, alcohol is used mostly as a beverage. Unlike most other drugs, alcohol is also a food. Wine and beer can be a part of a meal. Liquor is often drunk before or after a meal.

A Great Deal of Harm

Alcohol has been used widely in society for thousands of years. It was always known to be risky, though. In the thirteenth century, English philosopher Roger Bacon warned of alcohol's dangers. In his book *The Cure of Old Age and Preservation of Youth*, Bacon wrote, "If [alcohol] be over-much guzzled, it will . . . do a great deal of harm."

By the late nineteenth century, many people were very concerned about the safety of alcohol. They formed organizations called temperance societies. At first, these groups encouraged people to drink moderately. But soon they began to call for no drinking at all. In the United States and Canada, this movement was especially strong. The Women's Christian Temperance Movement was organized in 1874. In 1893, the Anti-Saloon League was formed. These groups called for a total ban on alcoholic beverages. The movement to totally ban or prohibit alcohol was called the Prohibition movement.

People who favored Prohibition believed that it would solve many of society's problems. Many of the leaders of the Prohibition movement were women. In those days, women had very little social or economic power. They mostly depended on men to earn money and take care of them. At that time, it was common for men to socialize in saloons. Companies that manufactured alcoholic beverages often owned or ran these saloons. They encouraged men to visit saloons and drink heavily and often gamble as well.

MAY I SEE YOUR ID, PLEASE?

In 1984, the United States passed a law establishing a national legal drinking age. That age is twenty-one. Before the national limit was set, states set their own age limits. However, this created problems. Often one state had a lower drinking age than a neighboring state. Young people would often be killed in accidents while driving back from a nearby state where they had traveled to drink or buy alcohol.

The law has saved lives, according to data collected by the US Federal Trade Commission (FTC). Since 1984, the number of high school seniors who drink alcohol has dropped from 66 to 42 percent. The number of traffic accidents involving youth has also decreased.

Prohibitionists argued that banning alcohol would keep men from getting drunk and abusing their wives and children. It would keep men from wasting their wages on alcohol. It would keep them from losing their jobs because they drank too much. Prohibitionists also hoped making alcohol illegal would reduce crime and accidents.

It took many years, but the Prohibitionists were successful. On January 17, 1920, the Eighteenth Amendment to the US Constitution went into effect. It banned the sale of alcoholic beverages in all states. (Canada had a similar ban. It was temporary, though, lasting for the duration of World War I.) This ban on alcohol lasted for almost thirteen years. This period was called the Prohibition era.

WOMEN FIND THEIR VOICE

Prohibition didn't stop people from drinking. However, the temperance movement did contribute to a major social change: the women's movement.

In the process of advocating for temperance, women honed their political skills. They organized and spoke at rallies. They published protemperance magazines and pamphlets. Women developed their voices and got the attention of the nation.

Many women worked both for temperance and women's suffrage. Suffrage is the right to vote. Women in the United States were not guaranteed that right until 1920, one year after the Eighteenth Amendment made alcohol illegal. Elizabeth Cady Stanton and Susan B. Anthony were leaders of the suffrage

(continued on the next page)

(continued from the previous page)

movement. Both of these women came to the women's movement from the temperance movement.

The temperance movement was sometimes called the Women's Crusade. And in some ways, the temperance movement *was* a women's movement. One of the major concerns of temperance leaders was that men who drank too much harmed their wives and children. Pointing out these problems also drew attention to how little power women had in society. When women took to the streets to demand better treatment as wives and mothers, they also demanded better treatment as citizens. They demanded the right to vote.

These members of a California chapter of the Women's Christian Temperance Union crusaded for a ban on alcohol.

Let's Try This Again

Prohibition didn't work out as many people had hoped. Many people, including women, wanted to be able to buy and drink alcohol. People were willing to buy it illegally. Making alcohol illegal created an opportunity for criminals to make a lot of money. Gangsters smuggled alcohol into the country. Then they set up bars and clubs where people could buy alcohol illegally. Al Capone was one of the most notorious gangsters who got his start during the Prohibition era. A complex network of crime developed as a result of Prohibition. It is still active today.

Before and during Prohibition, many people did abuse alcohol. But just as today, many people used it safely and moderately. Many adults drank alcohol at home or in restaurants. They enjoyed it in moderation with food. Most people were not happy with the law that banned alcohol. Finally the American people voted to make alcohol legal again. In 1933, the Twenty-First Amendment to the US Constitution was passed. It repealed the Eighteenth Amendment.

Americans agreed that alcohol could be dangerous. They agreed that children should not be allowed to drink. But they believed that responsible adults should be able to make their own decisions about whether or not to drink alcohol.

Making alcohol illegal did not solve the problems caused by alcohol. Indeed it caused many new problems. Making alcohol legal again didn't solve all these problems, either. How to safely and wisely use alcohol is a serious issue. Society struggles with this issue even today.

CHAPTER TWO

Alcohol in the Body

Alcohol is, for adults, a socially acceptable drug. Nonetheless, it is still a drug. Like many other drugs, it has short-term and long-term effects. Some of these can be very dangerous. Eventually most people will have to decide whether or not to drink alcohol. In order to make a wise decision, people need to understand what alcohol does to the body.

From the Glass to the Bloodstream

Alcohol is very quickly absorbed into the bloodstream. Then the blood spreads the alcohol throughout the body. Almost as soon as a person takes a drink of alcohol, the body starts trying to get rid of it. The liver begins to break down the chemicals in the alcohol. The liver can go only so fast, however. When there is more alcohol in the bloodstream than the liver can process,

Drinking too much alcohol can make it hard for someone to walk steadily or talk clearly. Young people are especially vulnerable to the physical effects of excessive drinking.

alcohol builds up in the body. This excess alcohol makes a person feel intoxicated, or drunk.

How much alcohol it takes to get drunk depends on many things. A person who hasn't eaten much will get drunk faster than someone with a full belly. A small person will get drunk more quickly than a larger person. Alcohol is a sedative—something that makes you feel sluggish or sleepy. Being tired can increase alcohol's sedative effect. Young people—kids and teens—experience alcohol's effects more intensely than adults. The digestive systems of elderly people often don't break down alcohol as fast as they did when young. This can make older people feel the effects of alcohol more intensely.

Alcohol is a type of drug known as a central nervous system depressant. (The central nervous system is the brain and the spinal cord.) This means that alcohol makes the nervous system respond more slowly. The body is always sending signals to the brain. Central nervous system depressants block some of these signals. When these signals are blocked, the body doesn't function as well. Walking and talking, seeing and hearing, and many other bodily functions are disrupted.

From Dangerous to Deadly

In very low doses, alcohol makes a person feel relaxed. Alcohol can, at first, make a person feel less anxious. Some people find this pleasant. However, a bit more alcohol can make it hard to concentrate. It can be hard to follow a conversation. It can be hard to express thoughts clearly.

Alcohol also affects coordination. It can be difficult to walk steadily. After a drink or two, a person is more likely to drop objects or knock them over. Spilled drinks are a common feature of a meal involving alcohol. Reaction time is also impaired at low doses, which makes it quite dangerous to drive a car or operate machinery.

People who have taken a slightly larger dose of alcohol might become drowsy. Their speech becomes slurred. Sometimes they say things that don't make sense. A drunk person's emotions can become exaggerated. They might become extremely friendly or sentimental. Some people become very talkative when they're drinking. Some become quick to anger.

At large doses, it becomes obvious that alcohol is a poison. People who have reached this point often vomit. This is the body's way of trying to get rid of the poison. Large doses can

Heavy drinking can cause someone to get angry and confront other people. These fights can become physical, so it's important to keep the person who is drunk away from others as much as possible.

dangerously lower a person's breathing rate. A person who has drunk lots of alcohol can pass out and even go into a coma.

One of the effects of alcohol is very sneaky. Even at low doses, alcohol can cause a person to make poor decisions. (This is why so many people choose to drink and drive.) Drinking alcohol dulls the part of the brain that realizes it might not be a good idea to drink more alcohol. The more one drinks, the more difficult it can be to realize that one is getting drunk. That means a single, small drink might not cause a serious problem in itself. However, it might be the cause of drinking more.

So what is the definition of a low dose of alcohol? There is no safe dose of alcohol for children and teens. The US Centers for Disease Control and Prevention (CDC) has found that youth drinking is a serious public health problem. According to the CDC, drinking contributes to more than 4,300 deaths of people under age twenty-one each year. Drinking also leads to thousands of emergency department visits each year. Any amount of alcohol is too much for young people.

NOT CREATED EQUAL

Alcoholic beverages vary in how much alcohol content they contain. That's why one serving of beer, say, is larger than one serving of wine.

Alcohol content is simply how much of the contents of the beverage is alcohol. This is called alcohol by volume (ABV). It is usually described as a percentage. The amount of alcohol in liquors is typically described as "proof." Proof is simply the ABV multiplied by two.

While some drinks are lower in alcohol than others, the difference is usually made up by serving size. Drinks with higher alcohol content are usually served in smaller portions.

Here are a few types of drinks with their ABVs:

Beer: Most beers and ales range from 3 to 10 percent ABV.
Wine: Wine is generally between 8 and 14 percent ABV. Fortified wines, such as sherry and vermouth, can get as high as 22 percent.
Liquor (or spirits): These have the highest ABVs (usually designated as proof). They typically range from 20 to 70 percent ABV.

However, most adults can drink small amounts safely. According to the USDA dietary guidelines, adult men should have no more than two drinks a day. Adult women should have no more than one drink per day. One drink is 1.5 ounces (44 milliliters) of liquor, 5 ounces (148 mL) of wine, or 12 ounces (355 mL) of beer.

After Effects

The effects of alcohol on the body aren't over once a drinker sobers up. The long-term effects of regular alcohol use are less obvious than the immediate effects. But they are no less serious.

There are many types of spirits, some with a very high alcohol content. Whiskey, of the various kinds shown here, is the most popular type of liquor in the world.

The best-known long-term harm of drinking is liver damage. Scar tissue builds up when the liver has to process too much alcohol. This illness is called cirrhosis. Cirrhosis of the liver can be deadly.

Alcohol can contribute to other deadly diseases. Acetaldehyde is one of the chemicals produced when the liver breaks down alcohol. This chemical is known to cause cancer. Many cancers are associated with regular alcohol use. Some of these are cancers of the mouth, throat, breast, colon, and rectum. The risk of cancer is even higher in people who both drink and smoke. Heavy drinking can cause blood clots. Blood clots can lead to heart attacks or strokes. Heavy drinking and binge drinking can also cause the heart to beat irregularly. Drinking also weakens the immune system. A weak immune system makes it easier to catch infectious illnesses.

Addiction is one of the most serious long-term effects of drinking. People can become addicted to alcohol just as they can to many other drugs. When people become addicted to alcohol, they find it very difficult to stop drinking. Even though they know the risks, they still drink.

Being addicted to alcohol is called alcoholism or alcohol use disorder (AUD). When people first start drinking alcohol, they may drink because their friends do. They may drink because they like the way it makes them feel. They may drink because it keeps them from thinking about their troubles. But soon the alcohol causes many new troubles.

When people are addicted to alcohol, they are unable to stop using alcohol. Sometimes a person is physically addicted to alcohol. Their body has become dependent on alcohol. People who are physically addicted feel sick when they don't have alcohol in their systems. When someone is psychologically addicted to alcohol, they might feel lonely, depressed, or anxious when they aren't drinking. It is important to remember that alcoholism is an illness. It is not a weakness of character.

The following are a few signs of alcohol addiction. No one of these signs means a person has an alcohol problem. But showing several is a warning that a person may have a problem.

- Missing or avoiding social or school activities and events
- Being moody and behaving in unusual ways
- Getting upset or angry easily
- Often being sick
- Having memory problems
- Telling lies or being secretive

According to the National Institute on Alcohol Abuse and Alcoholism (NIAAA), kids who start drinking before age fifteen are much more likely to one day become alcoholics than people who wait until they're adults to try alcohol. Alcoholism is a serious illness. Fortunately, health professionals have many ways to help people with alcoholism.

Underage drinking also damages the brain. The body is mostly grown by age twenty or so. The

Depression can have a variety of causes, including AUD, which may damage a young brain. Alcoholics often feel isolated from others as well.

brain keeps developing until the late twenties or even thirty years old. When young people drink heavily, some of their brain cells are destroyed. These brain cells are involved with learning, memory, and decision-making, among other things. This damage can be permanent.

For Adults Only

For adults, however, alcohol is not all bad. It can have some benefits. Most doctors agree that moderate drinking can be good for the heart. Red wine, in particular, has been shown to improve heart health. On the other hand, medical evidence suggests that even a small amount of drinking can raise one's risk of cancer at least a little bit. Scientists are still working to determine the balance between risk and benefit when it comes to alcohol use.

However, any benefits of alcohol are only for adults. No amount of any kind of alcohol is safe for children and teens. Even when it comes to adults, the safe amount of alcohol is probably lower than most people think. In 2018, a study published in the medical journal the *Lancet* looked at health and drinking in 195 countries. These researchers concluded that there was no safe level of alcohol use for anyone of any age. Not all experts agree with that. It may well be that small amounts of wine are not dangerous for adults. However, all experts agree that there is no safe level of alcohol for children and teens.

CHAPTER THREE

Alcohol in the World

Alcohol can cause plenty of health problems. The effects of alcohol on the body aren't the only dangers, though. Misuse of alcohol can cause problems with family, friends, and society, too. When making decisions about alcohol use, people have to think about the consequences to the rest of the world. Some of these consequences aren't always obvious at first.

Accidents and Anger

Drunk driving is one of the biggest dangers of alcohol. The CDC reports that in the United States someone dies every fifty minutes in a traffic accident involving a drunk driver. The people who are killed aren't necessarily the people who made the poor decision to drink and drive. Innocent people are often killed by drunk drivers. Sometimes the drunk driver survives a collision that

Police officers often use breath alcohol testing devices, like the one shown here, to tell if someone is driving under the influence of alcohol.

killed others. When this happens, the driver can be convicted of manslaughter. This can result in many years in prison. That driver also has to live with knowing that his or her poor judgment cost other people their lives.

Even when no one is harmed, driving while intoxicated is a serious crime. People convicted of driving while drunk have to pay hefty fines. They may lose their license to drive. In some cases, people convicted of driving while drunk have to spend time in jail.

Alcohol can also increase the risk of sexual assault. The National Institutes of Health (NIH) reports that alcohol is a factor in about half of sexual assaults in the United States.

Alcohol can cause the person who commits the assault to lose control of his or her actions. Being drunk can make it difficult for the victim to defend himself or herself. Alcohol can lead to other types of violence, too. Some people become more aggressive when they drink. Alcohol can make it more difficult to control emotions. When one of these emotions is anger, violence can be the result.

ALCOHOL BEHIND THE WHEEL

Driving while drunk is obviously a bad idea. It might not be as obvious, but driving while even a little bit drunk is dangerous, too. In order to drive safely, the brain and body must work together smoothly. Alcohol messes with that partnership. Here are a few of the reasons why.

- Alcohol lowers reaction time. A car pulls out in front of you. The driver ahead slams on the brakes. When these things happen, you have to respond quickly. Alcohol makes that hard to do.
- Alcohol affects vision. Drinking can cause blurred vision and make it more difficult to see, especially at night.
- Alcohol makes it hard to concentrate. Drunk drivers can't stay focused on the road. They can also become sleepy while driving.
- Alcohol interferes with judgment. How fast should you drive? Should you slow down or try to make it through that light? Should you be driving at all? Drinking makes all these judgments more difficult to make.

The Family Disease

Alcoholism can cause serious problems in families. When one member of the family has an alcohol problem, the entire family is affected. That's why alcoholism is often called a family disease. People who have alcohol problems may miss work a lot. This can create financial hardship for the family. People who drink heavily are more likely to have other health problems. Taking care of these health issues can be expensive. Alcoholism can add to family stress in other ways, too.

Alcoholics often avoid or miss social events. Alcoholic parents sometimes don't attend school programs or miss meetings with teachers. They may not show up for their children's birthday parties, recitals, or sports events. Often people with AUD can't be depended on to keep their promises. Alcoholic parents may love their children very much. But alcoholism has taken over their lives.

Parents with AUD can sometimes be distant from their children or other family members. People who are intoxicated may say things they don't mean. That doesn't stop the words from being hurtful.

A kid whose parent has a drinking problem can feel guilty about her parent's AUD. She may think she is the reason her parent drinks too much. This is not true, but it can be hard for some kids to realize they are not at fault. Children of alcoholics can also be very anxious. They worry about their parents getting sick, injured, or arrested. They worry that their parents will become violent. They may worry that outsiders will find out about their parents' behavior.

Many times, children of alcoholics have trouble having close relationships. Because their parents let them down, they don't trust anyone.

Growing up with a parent who has a drinking problem is very difficult. A child of an alcoholic can feel responsible for her parent's actions and desperate to stop the behavior from getting worse.

Sometimes kids with alcoholic parents will try to take on some of the responsibilities their parents are neglecting. They may feel they have to be the adult in the family. They help take care of the other children. They may have to do more chores than kids in other families. This can make it difficult for them to take care of their own responsibilities. Growing up without these worries is important. Children need to be able to concentrate on schoolwork and friendships. Kids need time to play and daydream.

Trouble at home can make it difficult for children to do well in school. They may miss school a lot, receive bad grades, or get in trouble. On the other hand, sometimes kids of parents with AUD will try to make up for problems at home by being an overachiever. This can be good, but it can also hide emotional problems that may not show up until years later.

Sometimes children and teens are the ones with drinking problems. Parents of kids with AUD often spend time focusing on the child with the problem. This can make other children in the family feel neglected. The kids who don't drink may get in other kinds of trouble as a way to get their parents' attention. Kids who drink often put pressure on their siblings to drink, too.

People with alcohol problems usually try to keep their excessive drinking secret. Keeping secrets can be hard on families. Children may not feel comfortable inviting friends home. Children of alcoholic parents often worry about teachers or other authorities finding out about their parents' problem. They may fear that they will be taken away from their parents. Kids who drink may expect their siblings to help hide their drinking from parents and teachers. All of these secrets and worries can put an enormous burden on individuals. It is also a huge stress on the family.

People who abuse alcohol often isolate themselves from their families. Kids who drink are especially likely to shut themselves off from their parents and siblings. This isolation makes it difficult for the family to help their loved one who has an alcohol problem. It also makes it hard for the person with the problem to ask for help when he or she needs it.

Down the Road

The health effects of alcohol can be short term and long term. So can the social effects. Kids with drinking problems usually do poorly in school. Bad grades can make it difficult to get into college or a career training program. Alcoholics often neglect friendships and other personal relationships. When they need support, they may find that they don't have many friends to turn to. Having close relationships is good for a person's physical and mental health. Damaging or neglecting relationships can lead to problems years into the future.

DOS AND DON'TS

Do wait until you are grown up to try alcohol.
Don't let friends convince you that drinking is cool, that it will make you seem more adult, or that you have to drink to have friends. None of this is true.

Do practice saying no to friends who might pressure you to drink. Have some answers ready.
Don't wait until you're in that situation to decide how to deal with it.

Do seek reliable sources of information and learn all you can about alcohol and its effects and consequences. The more you know about alcohol, the easier it is to make good decisions.
Don't just believe what your friends tell you.

Do ask for help from a trusted adult, such as a parent, teacher, or your doctor if you can't stop drinking.
Don't try to deal with AUD on your own.

Do ask for help from a trusted adult if someone you love has a drinking problem.
Don't try to solve the problem without professional help.

A conviction for driving while under the influence of alcohol can remain on a person's record for years. This can make it harder to get a job, get into college, or buy a house. These negative outcomes can affect someone's ability to have an independent and productive life.

CHAPTER FOUR

Staying Safe

People often think that AUD is some kind of character flaw. This is not true. People who abuse alcohol are not weak. They do not lack willpower. They have a disease. There are many rehabilitation programs and health care professionals who can help individuals and families learn to cope with AUD and get control of their lives.

Taking Steps

Even though AUD is an illness, it's not one you can prevent with a vaccination or cure with a pill. Over the years, there have been many approaches to treating alcoholism. In 1935, two Ohio men, Bill Wilson and Bob Smith, formed an organization to help alcoholics recover from their illness. Wilson was a businessman whose drinking had ruined his career and damaged his marriage. Smith was a physician looking for a better way to treat people like Wilson. The group became known as Alcoholics Anonymous, or AA for short. AA is active worldwide today.

All around the world, people with AUD turn to Alcoholics Anonymous (AA) for support as they work to stop drinking and stay sober.

The group is free to anyone who needs help with a drinking problem. As the name says, one of the rules of the group is that members are able to keep their identities private. Being anonymous was more important in the early days of AA. Back then, many people believed that alcoholism was a character flaw. Today most people understand that alcohol abuse is an illness. Still, most people prefer to keep their health issues, whatever they are, private. In AA meetings, members introduce themselves only by their first names, or first name and last initial. Bill Wilson was known as Bill W. In 1999, *Time* magazine named Wilson one of the hundred most important people of the century. The magazine called him Bill W.: The Healer.

The central idea of AA is that people who are struggling with a drinking problem can help each other recover. AA is a support group, rather than a medical rehab program. The organization is run by recovered alcoholics who want to help others overcome their drinking problems.

AA is a twelve-step program. Members follow a sequence of steps that help them eventually stop drinking. These steps involve acknowledging a higher power. (The higher power does not have to be God, however.) Some of the steps require making amends for harm caused by one's drinking. Many people have followed the AA program to overcome alcoholism. Over the years, many other programs have been created based on AA's twelve steps. Some of these help people with other addictions, such as to drugs or gambling.

Twelve-step programs are still very common. Now, however, there are many alternatives. Many types of behavioral therapy have been successful in helping people with drinking problems. With behavioral therapy, patients meet regularly with a counselor. The counselor helps patients understand and change their drinking behaviors. In many cases, people with AUD have other mental health illnesses as well. They may suffer from depression or anxiety. They may have post-traumatic stress disorder (PTSD). These issues can be treated as a part of their AUD treatment. Hospitals now offer in-patient treatment programs for people recovering from alcohol addiction.

For some patients, medications can be used to treat AUD. Medicines can't cure the illness. However, for some people, they can help control drinking. Taking medicines to control drinking can provide time to work on behavioral therapies. After a while, the patient may no longer need to take the medicine.

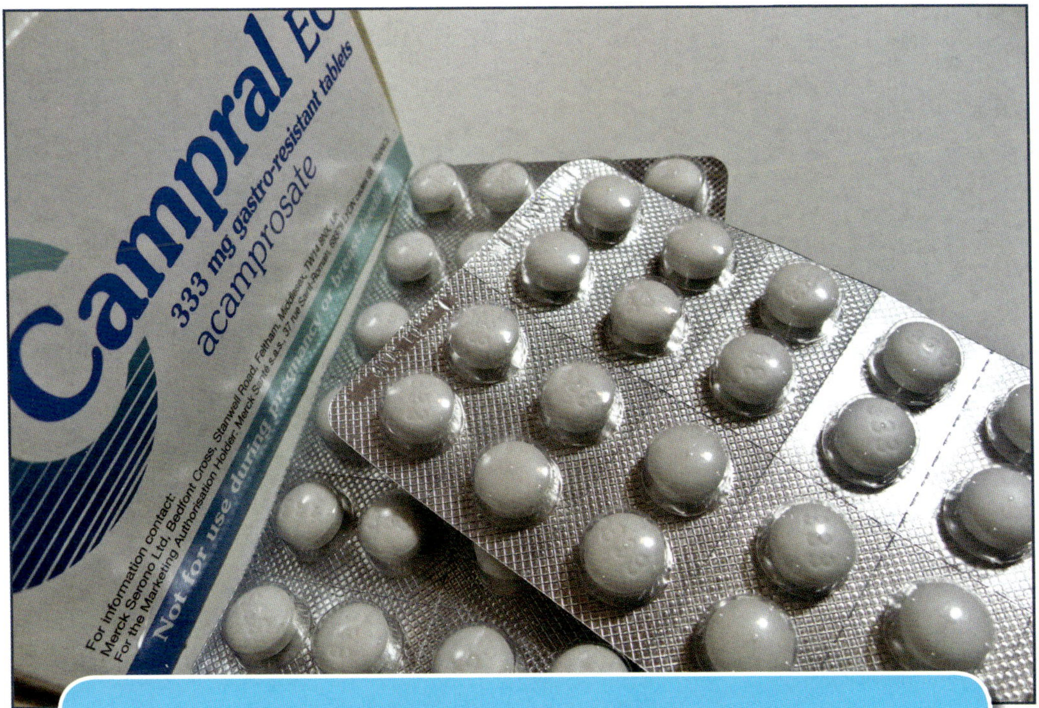

Campral is one of several medications designed to decrease an alcoholic's craving for alcohol. It is meant to be used along with behavioral therapy and a strong support network.

Helping the Whole Family

Alcohol problems can be extremely hard on families. That means the family members of people with drinking problems need help, too. There are many programs designed to help children, spouses, and siblings of alcoholics. When the person with AUD is getting treatment, it can be useful for family members to attend counseling sessions, too. One of the most common reasons people with AUD seek help is because they want to improve their relationships with their families. This is much easier when the family gets counseling together. Al-Anon and Alateen are two very useful programs for families of alcoholics.

Family therapy can be helpful for those struggling with AUD. Therapy also offers support to relatives who have been affected by their loved one's drinking problem.

Families can get help even when the person with AUD is unwilling. Children whose parents or siblings have AUD can benefit from counseling. Counseling can help family members with their own problems that have been caused by their loved ones' drinking. Talking with a counselor can help in other ways, too. Family members may learn ways to help their loved ones. It is very important that family members are able to express their own feelings about the situation. Professional counselors can help families do this in safe, constructive ways.

Many treatment programs and support groups are specifically designed for children and teens. They can help kids with AUD or kids with family members who have AUD.

RELIABLE RESOURCES

If a friend or family member is struggling with alcohol abuse, it can sometimes be hard to find dependable information and trustworthy advice. Here are several places to go for information and help that you can trust:

- **Just4kids:** 1-888-554-2627, http://nacoa.org/families/just-4-kids: A place for kids whose parents drink too much.
- **The Cool Spot:** http://thecoolspot.gov. A US Department of Health and Human Services (HHS) website with kid-friendly graphics, information, and links to other resources.
- **Alateen:** (757) 563-1600. An organization that offers help and support to families and friends of people with alcohol abuse problems.
- **SAMHSA's National Helpline:** 1-800-662-HELP (4357). Another HHS-sponsored site with free, confidential, information in English and Spanish, this help line offers support for people with substance abuse problems and their friends and families.

Sometimes a person believes that a family member needs help for a drinking problem, but that person doesn't want help. It can be hard to know what to do. Family physicians are a great place to turn. Doctors are trained to evaluate situations like these. They can determine what the appropriate type of help might be and offer advice about the best way to seek that help. Sometimes consulting a doctor is not an option. In those cases, school guidance counselors, teachers, or spiritual leaders can be helpful.

There are many options for treating AUD. There are many options for helping families cope with alcoholism. But in order to get help, someone must first reach out.

Just Don't Go There

Ideally, of course, people won't develop AUD in the first place. One of the best ways to avoid AUD and the many other problems associated with drinking is to wait until adulthood to try alcohol. For some people, that's easier said than done. Kids and teens often feel a lot of pressure to drink. Friends pressure each other to wear a certain kind of clothes or listen to a certain kind of music. That can be frustrating, but it's usually harmless. When friends pressure each other to drink, that's very dangerous.

It can be very hard to resist this pressure. People give in because they don't want others to make fun of them. They don't want to lose friends. Sometimes people say yes when they'd rather say no. But in order to stay safe and have a good life, kids need to respect themselves enough to say no.

Some kids find that it helps to have a response ready for when others try to get them to try alcohol. They might say something like, "I'm training for a 5K race, so I don't drink." Or they could say, "I have a test tomorrow and need to study tonight." Saying "I'm just not into drinking" is a great way to let others know it's a waste of time to keep piling on the pressure.

However, often the best thing to do is simply say no. A quick, direct "no thanks" keeps you from getting into a debate. You don't want to drink; you don't have to justify that to anyone. Some people find the broken record strategy works wonders when resisting offers of alcohol. This method is simply repeating

You don't need to make excuses for not wanting to drink, but if it makes you feel more comfortable, you can say you are training for a 5K race or some other sports competition.

the refusal. No matter what someone says, you just respond with "no thanks." You can also ask your friends for help. Saying, "I have decided to take care of my health and my life by not drinking. I'd love for you to help me with that" might turn peer pressure into peer support.

Learning the facts about alcohol can help people make smart decisions, now and later. Your family doctor, school guidance counselor, or librarian can point you to excellent sources of information and support. The important thing to remember is that you aren't alone. There are plenty of people and resources to help you.

GLOSSARY

ALCOHOLISM An illness characterized by the addiction to or compulsive drinking of alcoholic beverages.

ALCOHOL USE DISORDER (AUD) A chronic brain disease characterized by compulsive alcohol use and an inability to control alcohol intake.

ANONYMOUS When a person is not identified by name.

ANTIBIOTIC A medicine that kills microorganisms that cause illness.

ASSAULT A physical attack or the threat of physical attack.

COLON A part of the large intestine.

COMMUNION A sacrament in the Christian Church in which bread and wine are ritually shared.

CONVICTION A court's formal ruling of guilt.

COUNSELOR A professional trained in helping people with psychological or social problems.

CRUSADE An organized campaign to achieve a political or social objective.

DEPRESSANT A drug or other substance that reduces the responsiveness or effectiveness of the central nervous system.

FERMENTATION The process of turning carbohydrates or sugars into alcohol.

INFECTION Illness caused by the introduction of disease-producing agents.

INTOXICATED Affected by alcohol or drugs to the point where physical and mental responses are impaired.

MANSLAUGHTER The crime of killing someone without ill will or intention to kill.

PHYSICIAN A doctor or healer.

PROHIBIT To ban or forbid an activity or behavior.

RECTUM The lower part of the large intestine that ends at the anus.

REHABILITATION The process of recovering from a health issue, particularly alcohol or drug addiction.

RITUAL A religious or other formal ceremony in which certain symbolic acts are performed in a specified manner.

SHAMAN A spiritual leader who often uses alcohol, drugs, or magic to enter a trance state as a part of religious rituals.

SPOUSE A married person; one member of a legally married couple.

SUFFRAGE The right to vote.

TEMPERANCE Moderation in or abstinence from the use of alcoholic beverages.

FOR MORE INFORMATION

Al-Anon (Alateen) Canada
275 Slater Street, Suite 900
Ottawa ON K1P 5H9
Canada
(613) 723-8484
Website: https://al-anon.org
Facebook: @AlAnonFamilyGroupsWSO
Instagram and Twitter: @AlAnon_WSO
Al-Anon Canada provides support and assistance to families and friends of problem drinkers. It is free and open to anyone who needs help.

Al-Anon (Alateen) United States
1600 Corporate Landing Parkway
Virginia Beach, VA 23454-5617
(757) 563-1600
Website: http://al-anon.org
Facebook: @AlAnonFamilyGroupsWSO
Instagram and Twitter: @AlAnon_WSO
YouTube: Al-Anon Family Group Headquarters, Inc.
Al-Anon is an organization based on the twelve-step program of Alcoholics Anonymous. Families and friends of problem drinkers provide support and assistance to each other in an open and accepting environment.

Canadian Mental Health Association (CMHA)
250 Dundas St. West, Suite 500
Toronto, ON M5T 2Z5
Canada
(416) 646-5557
Website: http://cmha.ca
Facebook: @CMHA.ACSM.National/
Twitter: @CMHA_NTL
CMHA helps people and families in communities all across Canada get access to the resources they need to maintain and improve their mental health.

The Cool Spot
Website: http://thecoolspot.gov
This site is produced and maintained by the US Department of Health and Human Services. Featuring kid-friendly graphics and a wealth of information about alcohol use and abuse, it also includes links to sites of support groups for families and kids.

Mental Health America (MHA)
500 Montgomery Street, Suite 820
Alexandria, VA 22314
(703) 684-7722
Website: http://mentalhealthamerica.net
Facebook: @mentalhealthamerica
Instagram and Twitter @MentalHealthAm
MHA is a community-based organization that offers support services, including prevention, to Americans of all ages living with mental illness.

National Association for Children of Addiction (NACoA)
10920 Connecticut Avenue, Suite 100
Kensington, MD 20895
(888) 55-4COAS or (301) 468-0985
Website: http://nacoa.org
Facebook: @NACoAUSA
Instagram and Twitter: @NACoA_USA
NACoA is dedicated to supporting children whose lives are affected by alcohol in their families. They offer a wide variety of information, programs, and support. Just4Teens and Just4Kids are a part of this organization.

FOR FURTHER READING

Ambrose, Marylou, and Veronica Deisler. *Investigate Alcohol*. New York, NY: Enslow, 2015.

Burlingame, Jeff. *Alcohol* (Dangerous Drugs). New York, NY: Cavendish Square, 2016.

Connor, Leslie. *Waiting for Normal*. New York, NY: Harper Collins, 2008.

Henneberg, Susan. *Defeating Addiction and Alcoholism*. New York, NY: Rosen, 2016.

Hornik-Beer, Edith Lynn. *For Teenagers Living with a Parent Who Abuses Alcohol/Drugs*. New York, NY: Open Road, 2016.

Hyde, Margaret O., and John F. Setaro. *Drugs 101: An Overview for Teens*. 2nd ed. Minneapolis, MN: Lerner, 2013.

Landau, Jennifer. *Helping a Friend with an Alcohol Problem*. New York, NY: Rosen, 2017.

Landau, Jennifer, ed. *Teens Talk about Drugs and Alcohol*. New York, NY: Rosen, 2018.

Meyer, Terry Teague. *I Have an Alcoholic Parent. Now What?* New York, NY: Rosen, 2015.

Newell, Ella. *The Hidden Story of Alcoholism*. New York, NY: Rosen, 2014.

Peters, Jennifer. *Alcohol Abuse* (Overcoming Addiction). New York, NY: Rosen, 2019.

Sheff, David, and Nic Sheff. *High: Everything You Want to Know About Drugs, Alcohol, and Addiction*. Boston, MA: Houghton Mifflin Harcourt, 2019.

BIBLIOGRAPHY

Abbey, Antonia, et al. "Alcohol and Sexual Assault." *Alcohol Research & Health* 25, no. 1 (2001): 43–51. https://pubs.niaaa.nih.gov/publications/arh25-1/43-51.htm.

American Association for the Advancement of Science. "How to Save a Life." Retrieved February 8, 2019. http://sciencenetlinks.com/interactives/alcohol/ebook/pages/save-life.htm.

Bacon, Roger. *The Cure of Old Age and Preservation of Youth.* Translated by Richard Browne. London: M.L. Coll. Med., 1683. Retrieved February 1, 2019. https://quod.lib.umich.edu/e/eebo/A28790.0001.001?rgn=main;view=fulltext.

Borschel-Dan, Amanda. "13,000-Year-Old Brewery Discovered in Israel, the Oldest in the World." *Times of Israel*, September 12, 2018. https://www.timesofisrael.com/13000-year-old-brewery-discovered-in-israel-the-oldest-in-the-world.

Centers for Disease Control and Prevention. "Fact Sheet: Legal Minimum Drinking Age." Alcohol and Public Health. Retrieved February 1, 2019. https://www.cdc.gov/alcohol/fact-sheets/minimum-legal-drinking-age.htm.

Centers for Disease Control and Prevention. "Impaired Driving: Get the Facts." Retrieved February 1, 2019. https://www.cdc.gov/motorvehiclesafety/impaired_driving/impaired-drv_factsheet.html.

Cheever, Susan. "Bill W.: The Healer." *Time*, June 14, 1999. http://www.steppingstones.org/Time_Article.pdf.

Crocq, Marc-Antoine. "Historical and Cultural Aspects of Man's Relationship with Addictive Drugs." *Dialogues in Clinical*

Neuroscience vol. 9, no. 4 (2007): 355–31. https://www.ncbi.nlm.nih.gov/pmc/articles/PMC3202501.

Griswold, Max G., et al. "Alcohol Use and Burden for 195 Countries and Territories, 1990–2016: A Systematic Analysis for the Global Burden of Disease Study 2016." *Lancet* 392, no. 10152 (2018): 1015–1035. https://www.thelancet.com/journals/lancet/article/PIIS0140-6736(18)31310-2/fulltext.

Jouanna, Jacques. *Greek Medicine from Hippocrates to Galen*. Boston, MA: Brill, 2012.

McGovern, Patrick E., et al. "Fermented Beverages of Pre- and Proto-Historic China." *Proceedings of the National Academy of Sciences* 101, no. 51 (2004): 17593–17598. https://www.ncbi.nlm.nih.gov/pmc/articles/PMC539767.

National Institute of Alcohol Abuse and Alcoholism. "Underage Drinking." Retrieved January 22, 2019. https://pubs.niaaa.nih.gov/publications/UnderageDrinking/UnderageFact.htm.

Okrent, Daniel. *Last Call: The Rise and Fall of Prohibition*. New York, NY: Scribner, 2010.

Thadeusz, Frank. "Brewing Up a Civilization: Alcohol's Neolithic Origins." *Der Spiegel*, 24, December 2009. http://www.spiegel.de/international/zeitgeist/alcohol-s-neolithic-origins-brewing-up-a-civilization-a-668642.html.

US Department of Agriculture. *Dietary Guidelines for Americans 2015–2020*. https://health.gov/dietaryguidelines/2015/resources/2015-2020_Dietary_Guidelines.pdf.

Weiss, Elaine. "Women, Booze, and the Vote." *New York Times*, March 5, 2018. https://www.nytimes.com/2018/03/05/opinion/women-votes-feminism-alcohol.html.

INDEX